THE ADVENTURES OF
Scrappy
THE CAT

Jacqueline Ridge

MEOW!

I'D LIKE THAT KITTEN, PLEASE!

As a kitten, my fur was
BLACK.

I looked like most cats,
But David saw something
special in me.

As a kitten, I loved all the things that most kittens do.

Bird watching

Napping

Playing with
grandma

And keeping my black fur
Nice and clean.

LIFE WAS PRETTY NORMAL FOR ME...
UNTIL I TURNED SEVEN,

AND A VERY STRANGE THING HAPPENED.

SPOTS OF WHITE BEGAN TO APPEAR ON MY FUR.

At First I thought it was something I ate.

Or maybe it happened because
I always got into mischief.

Or maybe Grandma had given
me one too many kisses.

BUT IT TURNS OUT, IT WASN'T ANY OF THOSE THINGS.

SCRAPPY, YOU HAVE VITILIGO.

That's when I realised that
I wasn't an ordinary cat at all.

I was a SUPER CAT.

I HAD TO TEST MY NEW SUPER POWERS.

MY SPOTS GAVE ME EXTRA COURAGE
AS I WARDED OFF RODENTS.

Dogs were no match for me,

AND I CERTAINLY STOOD OUT IN A CROWD.

Best of all, the paparazzi loved me.

BUT, THERE WAS ONE NEMESIS
I COULDN'T SCARE AWAY:

THE BATHTUB.

I WAS SURE OF ONE THING.
THAT BATHTUB HAD MESSED WITH THE WRONG **Super cat**
FOR I AM

THE AMAZING
COLOUR-CHANGING FELINE!

I STAYED LOW,
CREEPING LIKE A NINJA
TOWARD THE BATHTUB.

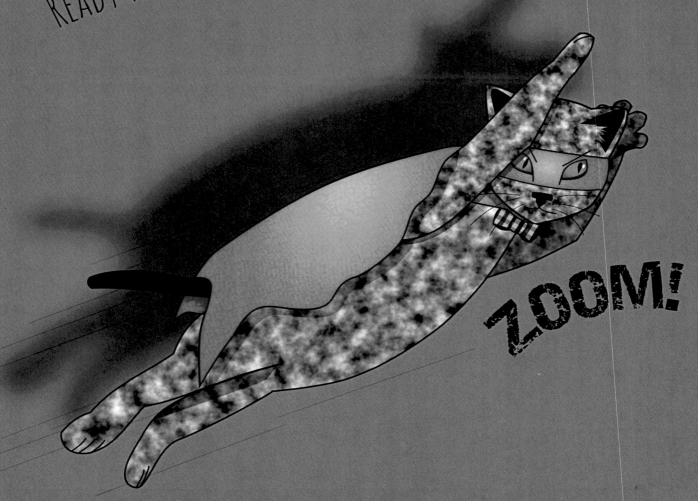

I STOOD BACK, EAGER TO SEE
THE DAMAGE I HAD CAUSED.

ACTUAL DAMAGE CAUSED

OH, NO!
I USED MY SUPER CAMOUFLAGE TO HIDE.

PHEW!

THAT WAS CLOSE.

I'LL LET YOU LIVE THIS TIME, BATHTUB,
BUT NEXT TIME,
YOU WON'T BE SO LUCKY.

About Scrappy.

Scrappy was born in 1997 with all black fur.

When he was seven years old, white blotches began to appear in his coat, changing his black fur to stunning marble.

His amazing transformation was attributed to vitiligo, an extremely rare condition for cats.

Scrappy passed away on the third day in April of 2017 after a beautiful life in the loving care of David and Grandma.

About Vitiligo.

What is it?

Vitiligo, characterised by the presence of white patches, is a condition in which the skin loses its melanocytes, the cells responsible for the skin's pigment. Skin, hair, retinas, or mucous membranes can be affected.

Is it common?

Vitiligo, though rare in cats, is much more common in humans. In fact, it is estimated that approximately 1% of humans are affected by vitiligo. It can affect people of any ethnicity, age, or gender.

Is there a cure?

There is no medically accepted cure for vitiligo, though treatment options exist that may alter the look of the affected areas of this typically lifelong condition.

Vitiligo poses no known health risks. Instead, it lets people see that you, like Scrappy, are

SUPER, SPECIAL, AND EXTRAORDINARY.

FOR GRANDMA.
— David

For Keira.
— aunt Jackie

Created in Memory of Scrappy.

73546991R00020

Made in the USA
San Bernardino, CA
06 April 2018